The Night Before Christmas

The Night Before Christmas

Clement Clarke Moore
Wendy Watson

Clarion Books · New York

FOR RUTH ASHTON

and for all my readers

Calligraphy on jacket and title page by Paul Shaw.

Clarion Books
a Houghton Mifflin Company imprint
215 Park Avenue South, New York, NY 10003
Illustrations copyright © 1990 by Wendy Watson

Library of Congress Cataloging-in-Publication Data
Moore, Clement Clarke, 1779–1863.
The night before Christmas / by Clement C. Moore ; illustrated by
Wendy Watson.
p.   cm.
Summary: The well-known poem about an important Christmas visitor.
ISBN 0-395-53624-3
1. Santa Claus—Juvenile poetry.   2. Christmas—Juvenile poetry.
3. Children's poetry, American.   [1. Santa Claus—Poetry.
2. Christmas—Poetry.   3. American poetry.   4. Narrative poetry.]
I. Watson, Wendy, ill.   II. Title.
PS2429.M5N5   1990   89-77661
811'.2—dc20   CIP   AC

HOR 10 9 8 7 6 5 4 3 2 1

'Twas the night before Christmas,
when all through the house

Not a creature was stirring,

not even a mouse;

The stockings were hung
by the chimney with care,

In hopes that Saint Nicholas
soon would be there,

The children were nestled all
snug in their beds,
While visions of sugarplums
danced in their heads,

And Mamma in her kerchief and
    I in my cap
Had just settled down for a
    long winter's nap;

When out on the lawn there
rose such a clatter

I sprang from the bed to see
what was the matter.

Away to the window I flew
like a flash,

Tore open the shutters and threw
up the sash.

The moon on the breast of the
new-fallen snow
Gave the luster of midday to
objects below,
When what to my wondering
eyes should appear,
But a miniature sleigh and
eight tiny reindeer;

With a little old driver, so lively
and quick,
I knew in a moment it must be
Saint Nick.

More rapid than eagles his
coursers they came,
And he whistled, and shouted,
and called them by name:

"Now, Dasher! Now, Dancer!
Now, Prancer and Vixen!
On, Comet! On, Cupid! On,
Donder and Blitzen.

To the top of the porch, to the
top of the wall!
Now, dash away, dash away,
dash away all!"

As dry leaves that before the
    wild hurricane fly,
When they meet with an obstacle,
    mount to the sky;
So up to the housetop the
    coursers they flew,
With the sleigh full of toys,
    and Saint Nicholas too.

And then in a twinkling, I
heard on the roof
The prancing and pawing of
each little hoof;
As I drew in my head, and
was turning around,
Down the chimney Saint Nicholas
came with a bound.

He was dressed all in fur, from
        his head to his foot,
And his clothes were all tarnished
        with ashes and soot;
A bundle of toys he had
        flung on his back,
And he looked like a peddler
        just opening his pack.

His eyes, how they twinkled! His
dimples, how merry!
His cheeks were like roses, his
nose like a cherry!

His droll little mouth was
drawn up like a bow,
And the beard of his chin was
as white as the snow;

The stump of a pipe he held
tight in his teeth,
And the smoke it encircled
his head like a wreath;

He had a broad face and a
little round belly
That shook, when he laughed,
like a bowl full of jelly.

He was chubby and plump,
a right jolly old elf,
And I laughed, when I saw him,
in spite of myself;

A wink of his eye,
     and a twist of his head,
Soon gave me to know
     I had nothing to dread;

He spoke not a word, but went
straight to his work,

And filled all the stockings,
then turned with a jerk,

And laying his finger
aside of his nose,

And giving a nod, up the
chimney he rose;

He sprang to his sleigh,
    to his team gave a whistle,

And away they all flew
    like the down on a thistle.

But I heard him exclaim ere
he drove out of sight,

"Happy Christmas to all and
to all a good night."